TEACHING

This book must be returned by
the latest date stamped below

12.06.16
11.12.18

Christmas with Tamworth Pig

CHRISTMAS
WITH TAMWORTH PIG

Gene Kemp

Illustrated by Carolyn Dinan

FABER AND FABER LTD
3 Queen Square London

First published in 1977
by Faber and Faber Limited
3 Queen Square London WC1
Printed in Great Britain by
Latimer Trend & Company Ltd Plymouth
All rights reserved

British Library Cataloguing in Publication Data

Kemp, Gene
   Christmas with Tamworth Pig
   I. Title
823'.9'1J   PZ7.K3055

ISBN 0-571-11117-3

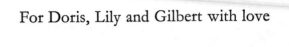

For Doris, Lily and Gilbert with love

"I shall give up causes for Christmas."

TAMWORTH PIG

"I hate Christmas. Scrooge is my favourite character."

HEDGECOCK

Chapter One

The end of term came at last.

> *"Build a bonfire.*
> *Build a bonfire.*
> *Put the teachers up on top.*
> *Put the prefects in the middle.*
> *Then we'll burn the blooming lot",*

sang Thomas, Lurcher and Henry as they ran home from school.

"Christmas is coming, the goose is getting fat," roared Henry, throwing his shoebag into the air.

"While shepherds washed their socks by night," bawled Thomas.

"All wearing pink pyjamas," shouted Lurcher. They threw their shoebags into the air. Lurcher's stuck in a tree.

"I don't care," he yelled. "I shan't want it for three weeks and then I'll send Podger to fetch it."

Lurcher had five brothers, all as tough as old boots, Podger the littlest. Once Thomas and Lurcher had been enemies, but now it was only occasionally that they had one of their battles.

"Cheerio," yelled Thomas and ran into his house, where

9

his sister Blossom had already arrived from school. She was a round, brown-eyed girl with a big grin and a comfortable disposition, which was a good thing as living with Thomas was rather like living near Mount Vesuvius; you never knew when the next eruption was going to happen. Blossom was showing her mother a Christmas card.

"You do like it, don't you? Honestly? Truly?" Her voice was anxious.

The front of the card had seven windows, which opened to show the Christmas story, drawn with loving care. Inside it was written:

"Love to Mummy and Daddy from Blossom, wishing them a very Happy Christmas."

"I think it's the prettiest card I've ever seen," said her mother and her voice had a funny catch in it, Thomas noticed. Most peculiar. But then, grown-ups always were peculiar.

"I've got one for you, as well," he bawled, digging down into his shoebag and pulling out a ball of old plasticine, the foot off an Action Man, several football cards, three plimsolls and a dirty sock, a water pistol, an old, brown apple core, half a stale bun, a paint-brush and a hair-ribbon.

The hair-ribbon he threw down in disgust.

"Ugh! I don't know how that got in there. What cheek! Some rotten girl has been poking around in my shoebag and leaving her horrible hair-ribbon in it!"

"Don't drop all your rubbish on the floor," protested his mother, but he *didn't* hear.

"Where is it?" he was muttering. "I know. It's in my

pocket. Here it is, Mum. It's a bit crumpled, but you don't have to mind that."

"Thank you, Thomas." His mother looked at the card. After a while she asked:

"Is it . . . is it a . . . Christmas picture?"

" 'Course not. I mean, everybody else in the class was doin' a Christmas picture, so I did one I knew you'd specially like."

"What . . . what is it?"

"It's my invention for converting manure, you know, farmyard muck, into fuel for cars and tractors. I knew you'd like it. It's jolly good. There aren't many Christmas cards like that, are there?"

"No," agreed his mother.

"And, look. I've written inside. Sorry the writing's a bit straggly."

"To Mum and Dad form Thomas. Cherry Christmas. What's a 'Cherry Christmas', Thomas?"

"Cheery, of course. You know. Ha ha, laughing. You are laughing, aren't you, Mum?"

"Oh, yes . . ." She sounded as if she were going to choke. At last, she managed to say:

"I'll put both cards on the mantelpiece. There."

Satisfied, Thomas went off to the kitchen in search of grub.

"I'm off to see Tamworth in a minute," he bellowed through a piece of cheese that he'd made into a sandwich with two chocolate biscuits.

A short while later he stood, full of admiration (and choclate biscuit), before a huge Christmas tree in Pig House.

It was the biggest he had ever seen in a room. Even Tamworth himself, the largest pig in Great Britain, was dwarfed beside it. Blossom was carefully unwrapping glass balls and tinsel from a cardboard box, and exclaiming

with delight. Thomas had brought Hedgecock and Mr
Rab with him. Hedgecock was in a crotchety mood
because Christmas was coming, and this was the season of
the year he most detested, so his feathery prickles were
ruffled and untidy, while his beady little eyes glittered
with malice. Mr Rab, on the other hand, poetical Mr
Rab, thought Christmas the most magical time of all.

"Ding, dong, merrily on high,
In Heaven the bells are ringing",

he warbled.

"We don't want them ringing here as well, then,"
grunted Hedgecock, kicking him. Hedgecock had never
been noted for his manners. Mr Rab moved round to the

other side of the tree, where he continued to sing softly, peering cautiously at Hedgecock through the branches.

"It's fantastic. Brilliant," Thomas said, looking up to the topmost branches.

"It's beautiful," beamed Mr Rab, still keeping clear of Hedgecock. "It has the true spirit of Christmas."

Hedgecock snorted.

"I think it's disgusting. Fancy uprooting a decent self-respecting tree out of the ground for all this Christmas tarradiddle. It will never be the same again. You ought to be ashamed of yourself, Tamworth Pig. I thought you believed in Saving Trees."

Tamworth wrinkled his long, golden snout at Hedgecock.

"In actual fact," he murmured gently, "the Friends of the Forest presented it to me, in recognition of my efforts on their behalf, and it is to be returned to its native wood, very carefully, after the Christmas season is over."

Hedgecock merely sniffed. Tamworth continued:

"I was pleased, as the piglets are coming home for Christmas and Pig House will look very jolly for them."

"Oh, smashing," cried Blossom. "All the twenty? Oh, super. Especially Albert. I do want to see Albert again."

Albert was the youngest and naughtiest piglet, the runt of the litter.

Hedgecock groaned.

"That gives us somethin' to look forward to, I must say. If that lot, especially Albert, are here for Christmas, then I shall hibernate in a dark cupboard."

"He doesn't mean it," cried Blossom, afraid that Tamworth's feelings might be hurt. "He loves them, really."

"Oh, no, I don't. The only things I love are numbers. Numbers never let you down. Numbers never talk stupid poppycock like that pink-nosed old fool on the other side of the tree, and there's no fool like an old fool. Everything except numbers is a load of rubbish. Numbers are the only thing that last for ever."

Mr Rab was just about to protest when Melanie, Tamworth's little black and pink wife, came in, with a bag of apples and a box of dates, and the room grew quiet except for the sound of munching jaws.

"I think I shall give up causes for this Christmas," Tamworth said, thoughtfully. "A brief respite should prove beneficial."

"I don't understand them long words," answered Hedgecock, "but I know the one good thing about Christmas is when it's over."

"Oh, you . . ." cried all the others.

Chapter Two

Blossom sat back with a sigh of satisfaction. She was surrounded by a sea of parcels, beautifully wrapped, labelled and be-ribboned, red and blue, green, silver and gold.

"There. Finished. They're all ready now. One for Mummy, Daddy, Tamworth, Melanie, Lurcher, you . . . Hey, have you bought me one yet?"

Thomas was playing a complicated game of Soccer in which he was trying to beat himself.

"What?" he muttered. Then he shouted, "Goal! Goal! Fantastic!"

"Have you bought me a present yet?" repeated Blossom.

"No."

"Why not?"

"I haven't bought anyone's yet."

'Why not?"

"Haven't thought about them yet."

"Well, there isn't long now. How much money have you got?"

"Eightpence . . . I think. Goal! Goal! Fantastic!"

"Eightpence! Why, I saved five pounds, nearly."

"Well, so did I. Then I spent it all on this game . . . oh!
FANTASTIC!"

"But what are you going to do?"

"Do? Play with it, of course, if you'll shut up for two
minutes. In the meantime, I'm going upstairs and then I
don't have to listen to you jabbering all the time."

And away he clomped up the stairs.

Hedgecock and Mr Rab were still arguing.

"How can you say that you hate Christmas?" Mr Rab
quavered.

"Very easily. I HATE CHRISTMAS."

"You can't mean it."

"Oh yes I can. All that awful cheer and goodwill, and
people stuffing themselves with food that nobody in
their right mind would ever eat. Like Christmas pudding.
Concrete mix with currants in. But even worse is being

expected to love everyone and give presents. Why on earth should I be expected to love someone I hate for all the rest of the year? Like you, for instance."

"You mean, miserable animal . . ."

"And don't think that I shall give you anything . . ."

"Well, you never do, do you, so it won't make much difference."

The two animals had to stop then, as Thomas pushed them both off the bed.

"You're playing this game with me," he ordered.

Meanwhile, Blossom wandered into the kitchen, where her mother was just placing some mincepies on a tray.

"Yummy! Can I have one?"

"Just one. And look out, they're hot."

"Mum," Blossom spluttered through her melting mincepie.

"Yes?"

"Thomas hasn't bought any presents and he hasn't got any money."

"Mm. Looks as if I shall have to give him a chance to earn some, then."

Blossom ran out to return with Thomas, Hedgecock, Mr Rab and the football game. They settled down on the floor and went on with the game.

"Thomas, have you got any money to buy presents with?" asked his mother, coming straight to the point.

"No . . . Oh! Goal! GOAL! Fantastic!"

"Thomas! Are you listening to me?"

"Yes. Oh! Goal! Shot! Brilliant!"

"Thomas. Thomas! If you don't stop playing that game I'll . . ."

At last, Thomas looked up, sighing heavily.

"What is it?" he asked.

"I think you'd better do some jobs to earn some money," his mother explained.

"I hate doing jobs."

His mother looked so furious that he said hurriedly:

"All right. Tell me what I've got to do. But I might as well be dead or in a dungeon."

Ignoring this, his mother said:

"First of all, my Christmas-flowering hyacinth needs watering. It's on the window-sill, and be careful with it, because it's coming along very nicely, and I want to have it on the table for Christmas Day. Use the old teapot for it. That will do."

Since he wasn't allowed to go on playing the football game, Thomas continued to play one in his head, as he watered the hyacinth.

"The centre-forward hurtles down the pitch, taking
the ball with him, but with fantastic skill Thomas gets
it away from him, and zooms down the pitch. No one
can get near him. The crowd roars, 'Thomas, Thomas', as
he heads the ball straight into the goal."

He went back to the kitchen.

"I've done that, Mum. What's next on the torture list?"

"Don't talk like that! Some children like to help their
mothers. Besides, you need some money. Go down to
the shop, and fetch me some more self-raising flour, as
I've run out. Shall I write it down?"

"No, dead easy."

"Hurry up, or the shop will be closed."

Thomas continued with his game as he ran to the shop.

"A packet of two-nil, please," he gasped.

"Now what do you really want?" asked Mrs Dyke,
who kept the shop.

"Some more flour."

"What sort?"

"Goal kick . . . no . . . I can't remember . . ."

"Plain, self-raising, wholemeal, cornflour?"

"Oh, plain, of course. Dead easy."

Blossom came rushing into the kitchen.

"Mum, please come. Your hyacinth is turning brown and curling up."

"Oh, no."

They looked at the Christmas-blooming hyacinth that was not going to flower for Christmas after all. Mum sighed and brushed her arm across her eyes, then stooped and picked something up off the floor.

"Why," she cried, "that's the old petrol can, the one your father kept weedkiller in, last year. That's what has killed my flower!"

Sadly, they returned to the kitchen, just in time for Thomas, still shouting: "Goal! Goal! Fantastic!" to crash into Blossom and send them both hurtling to the sink. This proved too much for the bag of flour, squashed between them. It burst open, puffing out white, feathery clouds over them, and over most of the kitchen.

"It looks like being a White Christmas," snorted Hedgecock, sitting covered in flour, looking as if he'd grown suddenly very old in the space of seconds.

Chapter Three

"*While shepherds watched their turnip tops*
    All boiling in the pot . . ."

sang Thomas.

"I wish you'd shut up," said his father wearily, putting down his newspaper. "You've been singing ever since I came in, and it's a horrible noise, truly horrible."

"I'm practising for the carol-singing tonight."

"Well, take care not to sing like that or you'll get boots thrown at you, instead of money given to you."

He picked up the paper and retired into it. Blossom looked up from the Chinese lantern she was making.

"I didn't know you were going. So am I."

"Who with?"

"The Vicar's wife and Mrs Postlewaithe are taking some of the girls from our glass."

"Ugh! Is Gwendolyn Twitchie going as well?"

Gwendolyn was the only daughter of Mrs Twitchie, the Head Teacher, and Thomas hated them both with a deep and deadly hatred.

"Yes."

"Then I'd rather be me than you. *I'm* going with Tamworth and Joe, the shire horse, Fanny Cow, Barry Mackenzie Goat, Lurcher and Henry."

If Blossom's eyes could have changed colour, they would have gone green with envy; instead, they rounded into soup plates.

"I wish I was going with you."

"Well, you could've if you hadn't been going with those rotten girls. I was going to ask you. Bet you have a rotten time."

Dad peered warily out from his newspaper.

"Are you saying that there are going to be two sets of singers out tonight?"

"Yes. Them and Us," answered Thomas.

"Why don't you come as well? And Mummy?" asked Blossom.

"No thanks. After all, someone's got to stay at home to put money in the collecting tins."

Up in the bedroom, Hedgecock was shredding paper towel all over the bed.

"What on earth are you making all that mess for?" asked Thomas.

"It's bad enough with that pink-nosed rabbity fool singing 'God rest ye merry, gentlemen,' all day long, when I don't want to be merry, and I'm no gentleman and never intend to be, thank you very much, but when I hear that the evening peace and quiet is to be ruined by hordes of carol singers, as well, then the only thing for me to do is to stuff my ears up and I can't find any cotton wool!"

"I have never in the whole of my life encountered such

a surly, ungracious animal as you," said Mr Rab, severely. "Life should be a shifting kaleidoscope of colour and joy."

"Shifting poppycock, you mean," shouted Hedgecock, ramming paper tissue into his ears and jumping up and down on the bed with fury. Then he rushed to the bottom of the bed and flung the blanket of knitted squares around him.

"One is a triangular figure," he continued to shout, "three is a triangular figure, six is a triangular figure . . ."

At seven o'clock, Thomas, Lurcher and Henry set out for Pig House, wearing football scarves and woolly hats, for the weather had suddenly turned very cold, so cold that their mouths blew puffs of steam as they talked and their noses tingled. A few flakes of snow drifted across their faces.

"Caw, look at that."

"I hope it snows and snows."

"A real white Christmas."

"Snow right up to the roof-tops."

"Snow all through the winter."

"No school."

"Mrs Twitchie dead in a snowdrift."

> *"Good King Wenceslas*
> *Knocked old Twitchie senseless . . ."*

they sang together.

They arrived at Pig House. Tamworth emerged, with a long muffler round his neck and a tin in his trotter.

'Home for homeless animals. Please give generously', read the label.

"Are we all ready?" cried Tamworth, to be answered by various assorted noises as Joe lumbered into view blowing clouds of steam, followed by Barry and Fanny. Thomas climbed on to Tamworth's back, Henry on Joe's and Lurcher on Barry's.

"Sqwark, sqwark, sqwaa-arrh-arrrrhhhhhhkkkkkkk," cackled Ethelberta Everready, the ever-laying hen, as she took a flying leap (or a leaping fly?) on to Joe's back, where she perched, cackling to herself from time to time.

"Giddy-up," Thomas cried, and away they trotted into the cold December night.

"A perfect night for carol-singing. Where shall we go first?" asked Tamworth, and the Vicarage was decided upon.

A few minutes later, somewhat breathless and chilly, they sorted themselves out before the Vicarage door.

Henry hauled his flute out of his football bag.

"Who brought the carol books?" asked Tamworth. But it appeared that no one had brought the carol books.

"Never mind, I'm sure that we know all the words," said the Pig, always optimistic. "Just give us a note, Henry."

The Vicar was sitting down to a quiet supper on his own. His dear wife had been practising all day, and the Vicar was not a musical man.

"This is nice and peaceful," he murmured to himself, taking his bowl of soup to a table near the fire, and settling down with an exciting murder story. At that moment an appalling screech rent the air. An extra large snowflake had drifted into Henry's mouth just as he opened it, preparing to blow. The Vicar paused, frozen, spoon half-way to his lips, when an even more bloodcurdling din made him drop soup and spoon straight on to his detective story. "O Come, All Ye Faithful" was being sung in Latin by Tamworth and in English by Thomas, backed by neighs, moos and grunts. High above this could be heard Ethelberta squarking the descant, while a pneumatic drill was singing, "O come, let's kick the door in." This was Lurcher who didn't know the words and couldn't sing in tune, anyway.

Shuddering, the Vicar hurried to the door and dropped a coin in the tin.

"Thank you, sir," Tamworth acknowledged. "Would you like us to sing another carol for you?"

"Oh, no, dear, no, no, no. If you will excuse me, I must go back inside as I have a lot of work to catch up with."

And he retreated back inside as fast as he could to his detective story.

"Whither next?" cried Tamworth.

"Baggs's farm?"

"No, I don't think so. Farmer Baggs, that good man, is not in this evening, and Mrs Baggs won't give us much of a welcome."

Farmer Baggs was the owner of Tamworth, and a friend of his, but Mrs Baggs detested Tamworth, and Thomas as well, for that matter.

"Let's go to my house," suggested Thomas. "Dad's waiting for us."

Yes, he was. The door opened before they could sing a note.

"I'll give you something, anything, providing you don't actually sing," said Thomas's father dropping a coin in the tin. "By the way, the other singers are also out. Listen. You can hear them."

They listened and through the night came the words ringing out clearly, "O Little Town of Bethlehem".

"*They* are very good. Why don't you go home? It's a very cold night."

"I think we shall do quite well," replied Tamworth, a little hurt.

At the next house no one came to the door at all,

though the lights were on. Someone inside turned the television on to full volume. At the next house, a woman opened the door and shouted, "Go away," extremely loudly and slammed the door shut.

"Let us not lose heart," cried Tamworth to his little band, who were looking a bit downcast. "It's for a good cause. Come on, let's go to your house, Lurcher, and see if your mother likes our singing."

As they arrived outside the Dench house, so the other band of singers appeared on the opposite side of the road. Blossom waved to Thomas, but he took no notice.

"Let's sing 'Silent Night, Holy Night'," Tamworth suggested. "People always like that one." Henry gave the note and they began. Tamworth was absentmindedly singing in German. No one else knew the words. An upstairs window was flung open.

"Shut up," bellowed Mrs Dench, shaking her fist at them. "The night is neither silent nor holy with you making that awful racket. Go home."

She banged down the window.

From the other side of the road came the sound of "Away in a Manger". They listened. A door opened.

"Thank you. That was really beautiful," they heard someone say.

Thomas and Tamworth looked at one another. At last the Pig spoke.

"There's an old saying that goes like this, dear lad. 'If you can't beat 'em, join 'em.' And I suggest that's what we do."

"All right. But I'm not going to stand anywhere near Gwendolyn Twitchie," answered Thomas.

28

Led by Tamworth, they went up to the others and asked if they could sing with them. The Vicar's wife smiled her welcome. Blossom shared her book with Lurcher. They all had their music and words, of course.

"See amid the Winter's snow," sang the Vicar's wife, her splendid voice soaring up to the sky. Everyone joined in, everyone in tune. More snow-flakes, fatter now, spiralled down.

On they went, singing the Christmas story. The animals backed with soft, gentle sounds. Into the tins fell coins for homeless people and homeless animals.

"Hot dogs and cocoa at the Vicarage," cried the Vicar's wife.

"Yummy, yummy," thought Blossom, lover of all grub, as she sang, "Noel, Noel."

Chapter Four

The days before Christmas are short, but they seem to last for ever. Thomas was busy doing jobs for people and, after his bad start, had managed to earn quite a lot, and so could think about the presents he had to buy. Blossom was helping with things in the kitchen, which made him cross, since he was much better than she was at cooking, or so he thought.

"You'd better go and play with somebody," she suggested when he offered to ice the cake with something different for a change. Thomas thought how snooty she looked, so he kicked her, then shot quickly out of the house, delighted to hear her yelp of pain and "Thomas, don't be so *mean*" following after him.

It was intensely cold outside, though no amount of snow had fallen yet, to his disappointment. But he still hoped for a white Christmas, for the clouds hung grey and heavy and a biting wind whistled round corners and up jumpers. Mr Dench, Lurcher's father, kept saying that it was going to be a hard winter this year; he could tell by the berries on the trees and the number of birds flying south. He'd sent all the Dench brothers out to collect firewood to burn on their old stove in case of power cuts.

Thomas pushed open the door to Pig House, to be met by warmth and comfort. Tamworth sat reading a newspaper, a cabbage on the floor beside him, and he took a bite from this from time to time. Thomas sat down on the floor and reached out for the pile of comics and paperbacks that Tamworth kept there for him. They read companionably, warm and cosy before the fire. Tamworth handed him an apple and they ate companionably together, as well.

"Do you know what a crunk is?" asked Tamworth, looking up from his newspaper.

"No."

"A reckling or a diddling?"

"No."

"A pepman, rinklin or nestlebird?"

"No."

"An Anthony or a runt?"

"Yes. I know what a runt is. Albert was one. A runt is the smallest and weakest of the litter."

"Yes, they're all names for the youngest littlest one of a family," explained Tamworth. "It's fascinating to discover how many different names the same thing can have."

"Yes," replied Thomas dreamily. "I've got lots of different names for Mrs Baggs. And Mrs Twitchie. Rotten ole ratbags, f'r instance."

He lay on the rug, dozens of really splendid names wandering through his head. He smiled.

"Beastly ole battleaxes. Disgusting ole dragons. Poisonous ole porcupines," he murmured.

At last he got to his feet.

"Please come shopping with me. I can never think what presents to give people. Last year I gave Dad a cigar and he doesn't smoke."

Outside, it had grown even colder. The wind had sharp needles in it, that drove through Tamworth's bristles and nipped Thomas's ears. He climbed on to the giant pig's back, and some of Tamworth's beautiful warmth came over to him. They went along in silence, for it was too cold to talk.

At the shop he bought quite a few things, helped by Tamworth, including a surprise present for Blossom that made him laugh inside. On the way back, Tamworth put him down outside his home, for it was growing dark and gloomy. The wintry evening was setting in as Tamworth returned to Pig House.

Thomas's house was full of lights and cases and coats, for Uncle Jeff and Aunt Cynthia had arrived: Aunt Cynthia tall, thin and spiky, Uncle Jeff tubby and jolly with a ginger moustache. Blossom was cuddling him.

"What's yellow, has twenty-two legs and goes crunch, crunch?" he asked her.

"A Chinese football team eating crisps. I know that one," laughed Blossom and they clutched each other giggling.

"Have you brought me a present?" asked Thomas, coming straight to the point.

"Now, now, little boys shouldn't ask questions," cooed Aunt Cynthia, waggling a finger at him.

"Why ever not?" he was just about to ask when he saw his mother's eyes fixed on him, so he just smiled instead. His mother had been a little crotchety ever since the flour bursting in the kitchen. Besides, they must have brought him a present. They wouldn't dare come to stay without a present for him, would they?

Later that evening, Thomas sat on his bed. It was now his turn to be surrounded by parcels.

"That lot's finished," he announced.

"They look awful," Blossom remarked. "Why did you use newspaper to wrap them up? It looks as if you're going to give everybody fish and chips."

"That's because you're fussy. Who cares what a parcel looks like if there's something inside?"

"I do. Taking off the wrapping is half of the fun for me."

Thomas counted them, aided by Hedgecock.

"I still haven't got enough," he said.

"Give away Mr Rab," suggested Hedgecock hopefully. "Think how nice it would be without him."

Mr Rab's nose turned pale.

"How can you be so unkind? You're a ... a ... monster, that's what you are. Now I shan't be able to write a poem for days."

"Thank goodness for that."

Tears began to flow down Mr Rab's sad, thin face. Blossom comforted him and he snuggled against her. Meanwhile, Thomas was shuffling round among his untidy parcels like a rummaging ferret.

"I need two more. One for Aunt Cynthia and one for Dad. I bought him a mug but it got broken somehow. Rotten luck."

He peered inside his cupboard.

"I can't think of anything. Can you? I know . . ." His face lit up with a wide grin. "I'll get some toothpaste and give her that. She must need lots of toothpaste as she's got such bloomin' great teeth."

He disappeared, to return rapidly with toothpaste and a bar of soap.

"Will this do for Dad?"

Blossom looked at it.

"He won't want Violet Scented Fragrant Special," she cried, amazed.

"Oh. Then I'll give the toothpaste to Dad and the soap to Aunt Cynthia."

"Thomas, you can't give Dad his own toothpaste for a present!"

"Bother. Why not?"

"Oh, don't be so *mean*. Go and buy them something really nice, tomorrow. If you haven't got enough money I'll give you some."

"All right," agreed Thomas.

"If I was ruler," Hedgecock ruminated, "I'd make it law that no one should ever give presents, and that Christmas should be done away with. I'd have a Maths day instead, when everyone would set everyone else Maths problems and we'd all have fun solving them . . ."

"FUN! You call that FUN!" screeched Mr Rab. "Why, I'd rather go to prison any day . . ."

"And that's just where you would go, you stupid, stripey thing, if you couldn't solve the problems. And there'd be no poetry. Any such rubbish would be banned."

Mr Rab drew himself up, quivering all over, thin paws twitching.

"In a land where poetry was no more, I should not wish to live," he said bravely. "Don't hit me."

But Hedgecock did hit him, until Thomas dumped him at the bottom of the bed, where he counted the coloured squares to himself, till he fell asleep, snoring.

Chapter Five

Gwendolyn Twitchie, dressed in a long blue gown, reclined on a sofa on the Church Hall stage. In her yellow ringlets sparkled a tiara and around her neck she wore a string of pearls belonging to her mother. A velvet coverlet was spread over her knees, and paper roses lay all around the stage. So did a number of bodies, fast asleep. Beside Gwendolyn, on bended knee, was Christopher Robin Baggs, Mrs Baggs's awful, spotty son. He was wearing purple knee breeches and a satin coat as yellow as Gwendolyn's curls.

She was Sleeping Beauty.

He was Prince Charming.

And they were loving every minute of it.

The Hall was thronged with admiring Mums come to see a Christmas pantomime arranged by the Vicar's wife. The school orchestra was providing the music, among them Blossom playing the violin.

At the back of the Hall were trestle tables covered with goodies for everyone to enjoy after the performance.

Also at the back of the Hall, as near to the food and as far away from the stage as possible, sat three figures, Thomas, Lurcher and Henry.

"*We're* only here for the grub," said Thomas.

However, they had to sit through the performance first.

"He's going to kiss her," hissed Lurcher.

"How horrible," breathed Henry.

Thomas made his famous sick noise, the one his mother had forbidden him to use in the house. Several Mums turned round.

"SHUSH!" they said.

Thomas, Lurcher and Henry bent over, heads nearly on their knees, red-faced, squirming, wriggling, trying to stop themselves laughing as the choir sang,

> "*He kissed her cheek to wake her up,*
> *Wake her up, wake her up . . .*"

Christopher Robin leaned towards the sleeping form. A couple of ringlets twitched in anticipation.

"Fancy kissin' 'er," hissed Lurcher.

"Fancy kissing him," whispered Henry.

Thomas made his sick noise again. Louder this time.

Angry faces turned to glare at them, and among them Thomas saw the face of Mrs Baggs, wearing a large green hat with orange and pink feathers on it.

"Stolen from one of the hens," he thought.

She was red with rage and Thomas was just about to put out his tongue at her when he saw that his mother had turned round too, so he sat up straight and concentrated on the play.

Christopher Robin kissed Gwendolyn.

Cheers and clapping were heard, and a voice calling: "What a load of rubbish."

"Shush," cried the Vicar's wife, hurt.

Sleeping Beauty woke up, yawning and stretching, then smiled at her Prince and shook her curls. Thomas closed his eyes. He could not bear to look. Now the King and Queen and all the Court were waking, yawning and stretching. There sounded a loud crash on the cymbal and in somersaulted Crasher Dench, the Court Jester.

"Creep," muttered Lurcher. "I can do that better than he can."

"Yes, I know. But you wouldn't want to, would you? Not with them," said Thomas.

"No, I suppose not," Lurcher agreed, but he felt like doing a really complicated series of handsprings down the Hall just to show them, all the same.

The pantomime drew to a close amid riotous applause. Sleeping Beauty and Prince Charming were married, and descended from the stage to parade through the Hall with two small pages holding her train; Podger Dench was one of them. Gwendolyn was radiant. This was her hour. She was the star of the show, with everyone's eyes upon her—or nearly everyone's eyes. Thomas had his screwed up tightly so that he couldn't see. From time to time he muttered to himself. But Gwendolyn walked on, a stately figure full of pride. She had always known that she was born to be a Princess and here she was, at last, taking her rightful place. With regal grace she moved slowly, all the cast following behind, to the tables at the back of the Hall, where two chairs had been transformed into thrones with the aid of red crepe paper and tinsel.

Lurcher was moving, his mind on the grub.

"Come on," he said. "Let's get a place. The best one's over there."

The three boys pushed forward and grabbed seats, eyes fixed on the delicious spread before them. Thomas looked longingly at a plate of fat, juicy pork sausages. He had promised Tamworth that he would never eat any, but they were very tempting. He took his eyes firmly away and stared at the other delicacies, for there were plenty, slices of chicken, hardboiled eggs, sandwiches, mincepies, crisps and so on. Oh, what bliss! He looked up to see if it was time to start eating.

And found that Mrs Baggs was just opposite, glaring at him with huge dislike, while Sleeping Beauty and Prince

Charming were moving into their thrones beside her, Mrs Twitchie and the Vicar following behind. Thomas gulped and turned to Lurcher.

"I can't sit here," he hissed desperately.

"Why not?" Nothing could put Lurcher off his food. He reached out a grimy hand for a sandwich, but Mrs Twitchie pushed it away.

"Let us rise to say Grace," spoke the Vicar.

In his worst nightmare Thomas had never imagined the faces of the greater part of his enemies lined up together looking at him, but there they were: Gwendolyn and Christopher in their royal robes, Mrs Twitchie in sequins and Mrs Baggs in her feathers. Thomas looked once more at the food he had fancied. He fancied it no more. He swung round from the table with one desire in his mind—to get away.

"For what we are about to receive," intoned the Vicar, "may the Lord make us truly thankful . . ."

Thomas, making his escape, pulled the white damask tablecloth, specially borrowed from Mrs Baggs for this occasion. It slid off the table, its smoothness jerking into a thousand rumples and creases. Thomas's chair crashed into Lurcher's, which toppled over, taking Lurcher with it. Crash, clatter, clink went the cups and plates: chunk, whoosh, sloosh went the food and drink. They all received it, the royal party, right in their laps, though they weren't at all thankful.

In the centre of it all, mouth wide open, sat Gwendolyn, her yellow curls wreathed in lemon jelly.

She started to scream just as Thomas reached the Hall door.

Blossom slipped quietly into Pig House.

"I thought I'd find you here," she said.

Thomas was curled up against Tamworth, his head resting on the great, golden side, his hands stroking the soft bristles. The pig was speaking in a deep and gentle voice.

"My great-grandfather was a famous pig of that era," he said. "He was called Sandy, and he lived on a farm, Shugborough Farm, in the middle of England. Very proud of him they were. He won many shows because he was such a fine figure of a pig. Hello, dear Blossom. What have you got in that bag, might I ask?"

"I brought some food. I thought we could have a jolly little feast, here. But go on telling us about your grandfather while I arrange it all out for us."

"Lots of Sandy's piglets emigrated to New Zealand, where there are many Tamworth Pigs today. Sandy himself did stalwart work in helping to get better conditions for animals in his area, and then, alas!"

"What happened?" asked Thomas.

"His owner, a fine man, like Farmer Baggs, died, and then his son was killed in an accident, and Sandy was sold to another man, a villainous creature who sold him in turn to a butcher named Starkey, and made into sausages and faggots."

Tamworth had gone pale under his bristles. Thomas patted him soothingly.

"To this day, the very word 'faggot' fills me with dread. Oh, such villainy. This butcher put a slogan outside his shop. It read:

'Sandy Pigs make Starkey Faggots.' "

"Shame!" cried Thomas, forgetting how much he had

41

fancied those fat, juicy sausages earlier. Tamworth shivered despite the warmth of the room.

"Never mind," comforted Blossom. "Look, I've put all this lovely grub ready for us, and it's all quite safe, Tamworth. There are no faggots here."

Silence fell as they did justice to the food.

"Where did you get it from?" asked Melanie, at last.

"That's a secret," laughed Blossom. Then she explained. "The Vicar's wife, who's always nice to us, specially Thomas, even when he's awful, sent some for him, and I kept my share to eat here, as well."

"I didn't mean to wreck that table," Thomas said slowly. "It was just all of *them* staring at me, and I had to get away. I don't often mean to do anything wrong. Things just happen, and then Mum gets mad at me. It isn't fair."

"Don't worry. Just take life as it comes, for there is no armour against Fate. Blossom, are you crying?"

Blossom's shoulders were shaking and she was having difficulty with a chocolate biscuit, which wasn't like her.

"No, no, I'm laughing. You're both being so serious, but if you'd seen Gwendolyn Twitchie covered in jelly you'd laugh too, because she's been awful for weeks and weeks, boasting about being a Princess. All the kids are pleased, even if Mrs Twitchie and Mrs Baggs aren't."

Thomas started to grin. Tamworth started to grin. Then they all started to laugh and soon Pig House was full with the sound of laughter.

And Mrs Baggs, returning home, heard their laughter and thought bitter, angry thoughts.

Chapter Six

Thomas and his mother were having one of their conversations.

"You're not going like that, are you?" she asked.

"Why, what's wrong?"

"You haven't washed your face or combed your hair, your shoelaces are undone, your sweater's back to front and your shirt's hanging out."

"What does it matter?"

"You must look tidy to go shopping with Aunt Cynthia."

Thomas made his sick noise.

"Don't you dare make that noise in the house. And be careful or she may hear you."

"I don't care if she does. I hate shopping. I specially hate shopping with her." He paused for a moment. "The only thing I can think of worse would be shopping with Mrs Twitchie or Mrs Baggs."

"They're like three witches," he thought. "Sent to haunt me."

"Thomas, you're not listening. Aunt Cynthia is buying you a new pullover and you can choose the one you like."

"But I don't want a new pullover. I like my old pullover."

"Oh, I give up. You—are—having—a new—pullover. Anyway, Uncle Jeff is going as well, so you may get something you do like. That is if you behave yourself."

"I don't know how to behave myself if she's there, because something always goes wrong."

"Well, just try, for once," his mother said, irritably.

Blossom came in, looking rather smart.

"I'm wondering what colour dress to choose," she said.

"Khaki with muddy spots on."

"Thomas, that's enough. Go and wash your face. Properly, this time. And tidy yourself up."

Thomas stomped away, muttering that he might as well be dead or in a dungeon. At last he came down again.

"Is that the best he can look?" enquired Aunt Cynthia, who had now arrived and was ready to depart on the shopping expedition. Thomas glared at her.

"Tie your shoelaces, and no, you're not taking Hedgecock and Mr Rab."

Once more he stomped upstairs. He plonked the two animals on the bed.

"Christmas has just got to be good to make up for this torture," he said.

"I've told you a hundred times, that Christmas just isn't worth putting up with what you have to, to get there," Hedgecock remarked.

"I shall compose a Christmas poem while you're gone," offered Mr Rab.

Hedgecock groaned. "I knew when I woke up that this was going to be a rotten day. All right, then I shall think up some number tricks."

"Are you coming?" called a voice from below.

Thomas ran downstairs, landing on every third step. Aunt Cynthia shuddered. At last, they settled into Uncle Jeff's car. Mum waved them off with an air of relief.

It wasn't far to the nearest town, but Thomas always felt sick in that car. It was Aunt Cynthia's smell; Wild Musk Blossom said it was called. Even worse, she'd lent some to Blossom, who sat there ponging of Odour of Rotten Eggs or whatever it was. As if this wasn't bad enough, they were having a snobby conversation about shops and prices and clothes and wouldn't it be wonderful to go skating.

"I'm going to be sick," he announced loudly and clearly. "Open the window."

He didn't really think that he was going to be, but he wished to get rid of both the scent and the conversation. An icy wind whirled into the car as he wound down the window to the bottom.

"Close that window," shrieked everyone else.

He did so, reluctantly. Aunt Cynthia drew herself up in her seat belt.

"I'm beginning to think it was a mistake to bring him."

"I don't want a pullover and I was going to go to the woods with Tamworth today, to see if we could get a sprig of holly."

"You'll have to make the best of it, old man," replied Uncle Jeff. "But if we get on with this shopping, we can come back early, you can go to the woods and I can go to the Duck and Drake."

"Oh, no, certainly not. We're having lunch in town. We'll go somewhere smart. It will be a nice change for Blossom."

Thomas curled up in a miserable heap in the corner of the car. This was going to be even worse than he had supposed.

At last they arrived, and parked the car with some difficulty, for the town was full of people doing their Christmas shopping. As they got out, Aunt Cynthia and Thomas looked at one another and, funnily enough, their thoughts were almost identical. She thought:

"Doesn't he look dreadful?"

He thought:

"Doesn't she look awful?"

Thomas's shoelaces were still untied and he'd managed

46

to tear at his coat pockets so that they were hanging loose. Aunt Cynthia was wearing her best fur coat. Thomas hated anyone who wore the skins of dead animals, a pink hat with petals on it, and a pair of high red boots.

"She looks like Puss in Boots gone mad. I hope I don't meet anyone I know," he thought miserably. And the long torture began. Blossom and her aunt stopped at every window, comparing prices. Then they trailed round shop after shop, trying on dress after dress.

"How do I look?" asked Blossom, once.

"Better in jeans," he snapped, and fell into a gloomy silence, while his uncle seemed pretty miserable, as well. At last he stopped and bought a paper, so Thomas bought a comic, and then followed the rest, his miseries forgotten in fun and adventure.

Suddenly he was seized and shaken.

"I thought we'd lost you," Aunt Cynthia shrieked. "I was terribly worried. And there you are, twenty yards behind, reading a comic, walking along in the middle of the pavement!"

"Twenty metres, not twenty yards," corrected Thomas. He thought perhaps she didn't know about metres. But she quivered like a nervous horse.

"Are you trying to make me look a fool?" she cried.

Thomas didn't know how to answer this peculiar question, but was saved by Blossom's crying that she'd found just the dress she wanted, at last, there in the window.

The dress was purchased and it was now his turn. Like one in a nightmare, he went into a shop where a large, beaming lady bore down on him, and he heard his aunt say:

"He's small for his age, you know."

"Just because she's eight feet tall, she thinks everyone else is small," he thought angrily.

Pullover after pullover was brought out. Only one he liked, a yellow and red one. No, that wouldn't do, it was much too common, said his aunt. Thomas withdrew all interest, all feeling, like a snail retreating back into its shell. At last they purchased a plain one of good quality that looked exactly like the one he had already for school. He couldn't see why anyone had bothered.

And now, lunch . . .

"Shall we go to the Red Lion?" Uncle Jeff asked hopefully.

"Not with the children."

"There's a children's room."

"No."

"Fish and chips?"

"No, I know where we're going."

She led the way to a cafe full of people just like herself, with fur coats, big hats and loud voices. While she studied the menu, Thomas rearranged the knives and forks and popped some sugar lumps in his pocket for Joe.

"Don't do that," she said sharply.

A bowl of soup was placed before him and Thomas ate it with gusto, for he found he was very hungry.

"Blossom, does your brother always puff and blow like that?" asked his aunt.

Thomas didn't know whom she was talking about. He took a look around.

48

Chicken and chips arrived; splendid.

"Can we finish it with our fingers like we do at home?" asked Blossom.

"Certainly not."

"I shall," said Uncle Jeff, "let's all cheer up, shall we? Blossom, how do you make an apple crumble?"

"I don't know."

"Drop it on the floor!"

Then, suddenly, right out of the blue, with no warning at all, Thomas sneezed. Right over the table.

"Oh, how disgusting . . ."

Thomas tried to say he was sorry, but he could feel another one gathering force in his nose . . .

"Next time, please turn your face the other way!"

Thomas did so, desperately. And sneezed all over a man sitting behind him at the next table. He stood up, got out his handkerchief, wiped his forehead, then bowed to Thomas and said:

"Thank *you* very much," and walked out.

Aunt Cynthia rose to her feet.

"This is too much for me. I'm retiring to the Ladies' Room, where I shall take an aspirin and rest. I shall see you later."

In the silence that followed, Uncle Jeff leaned forward and said:

"Suppose we all have a large helping of pudding each, and enjoy ourselves."

And they did.

Chapter Seven

The sun shone down from the palest of blue skies. Everything glittered; trees, houses, leaves, the grass they walked on, each vein, each line, each curve, each fold outlined in white. The grey, cold world of the last few weeks had been transformed to a land of magic.

Tamworth, Thomas, Blossom, Mr Rab and Hedgecock had set off, at last, on a holly-picking expedition, and they now ran swiftly through the frozen morning, their breath hanging in the air, their feet, paws, hands, noses a-tingle. Through the Rainbow Field they ran, over Hunter's Bridge on the way to the Tumbling Wood, so called because the trees grew on such a steep hill that it looked as if they were falling over.

"Is your snout cold, Tamworth?" asked Hedgecock. "Mine is."

"Yes, extremely so," Tamworth replied, wrinkling the very long object. Tamworth Pigs have longer snouts than other pigs, though wild boars have very long snouts, too."

"The area of your snout must be much greater than the area of my snout," continued Hedgecock. "I must work it out, some time. You must have a greater area of cold than I have."

"Yes, but I have more fat to keep me warm," said the Pig.

"Hurry up," cried Mr Rab, "your snouts aren't as cold as my nose." And indeed his nose shone like a cherry rather than its usual pink blancmange colour.

Just on the edge of the wood they paused, and looked at the white hills and fields that stretched out to the horizon.

"I wonder what the temperature is?" asked Thomas.

"Ninety degrees below zero," suggested Blossom.

"I doubt if it's that," Tamworth replied, "but it is unusually cold. As the poet said:

The owl for all his feathers was a-cold,
The hare limped trembling through the frozen grass."

"Ah, just so," cried Mr Rab. "We poets see everything in a clearer nobler light than other people."

Hedgecock kicked him.

"Stuff that," he said coarsely. "And Tamworth, I do wish that you wouldn't set him off. Poetry puts all sorts of ideas into his foolish head."

Mr Rab sat speechless, shaking with rage, when a voice was heard:

"Indeed to goodness, and how delightful it is to be seeing you, despite the coldness. Won't you enter my house, now?"

It was the Welsh Rabbit, Mr Rab's friend, so he went along with him to his home near the elderberry bush, while the others entered further into the frozen wood. The leaves of summer had long since gone and the nuts of autumn were hidden away in squirrels' dreys. All was

still and silent, as if under a spell. The trees seemed to be waiting for something that was about to happen.

"Perhaps they know that it will be Christmas soon," Blossom thought.

They arrived at last at the middle of the wood, where a giant oak tree reared its massive branches to the sky. Around it stood a ring of beech trees. Beneath them the grass sparkled with frost, and a little way behind them was a holly bush covered in red berries.

"We'll just take one branch," Tamworth said.

So Thomas cut off one branch very carefully with his knife. Hedgecock was counting away at tremendous speed.

"Ninety-eight berries," he gasped.

"I've found some mistletoe," Blossom called out. "I'll get some and we can hang it in the hall and then

Thomas can kiss Gwendolyn Twitchie under it. Owh! don't pull my hair. I didn't mean it."

"If you ever say anything like that again, I shall exterminate you," Thomas threatened, and he went on making angry noises for some time.

"Shut up and have some peanuts," said Blossom, getting a supply of food out of her pocket, and they all paused to have some.

"The Druids worshipped the mistletoe," Tamworth said. "Having it in our houses is a reminder of those times."

"The Druids were cruel and horrible, weren't they?" asked Blossom, half-way through a Mars bar.

"We really don't know a great deal about them, except that they were learned in the knowledge of that time, and the Romans were very wary of them."

"They burnt people in big wicker baskets," added Thomas. He smiled happily. "There are some people I should like to burn in a big wicker basket," he went on.

Blossom shivered. "Don't be cruel. It makes me feel peculiar inside."

"Now the Celts were a wise race. They worshipped the Pig, you know. A very superior animal they considered it. Which it is, of course."

Eating the last of the peanuts, they made their way back to the elderberry bush. Hedgecock suggested with a wicked gleam in his beady eyes that they leave Mr Rab behind. But he was just coming out of his friend's burrow.

"He is very busy down there. Making it snowproof, indeed to goodness . . ."

"Stop talking like him. It's bad enough when you talk

like you, but when you talk like him, it's worse," grumbled Hedgecock.

"I shan't say anything, now."

"Go on. Don't take any notice of him."

"My friend says that all the animals are saying that there's going to be a very deep snow indeed, and they're all snowproofing their homes."

"An enormous, deep snow?" asked Thomas.

"An enormous, deep snow."

"Yippee!" shouted Thomas.

Later that day, Blossom, who had been shopping, came running in, eyes shining.

"Come on. Everyone's sliding on the pond. It's frozen solid."

Thomas flung on his clothes as fast as possible and rushed out to the pond beside the Duck and Drake.

The Dench brothers had made a slide from one side of the pond to the other. Thomas and Blossom joined in and were soon flying along at terrific speed. Then Henry arrived, and Mr Starling, the teacher Thomas liked, with his little boy, who slid along on his bottom. At last Blossom paused for breath, face bright and beaming.

And who should come tripping up to the pond but Gwendolyn Twitchie, followed by Christopher Robin, as spotty and unlovely as ever. Gwendolyn began to lace on the most beautiful pair of skates. Then she teetered round the edge of the pond. Then, growing more confident, she circled into the centre.

"She isn't bad," Blossom thought enviously.

"I hope she falls flat on her conk," thought Thomas.

"I do a lot of skating at skating rinks. Proper ones," Gwendolyn said to Blossom as she paused for a moment. Then she began to perform once more. People stopped to watch her. Gwendolyn started to feel like a Princess again.

But all eyes forsook her when a splendid and unlikely figure appeared. Wearing a red woolly hat and little neat skates on his trotters, Tamworth executed a magnificent figure of eight in the middle of the pond. A cheer went up from the gathering spectators.

"Mind yer don't break the ice, Dad," sang out Deadly Dench, Lurcher's eldest brother.

Tamworth just smiled and bowed, then continued his swooping, turning and gliding, ears outstretched to the breeze, tail curled tightly behind him.

Chapter Eight

Late that night, after everyone was in bed, the wind stirred and shifted. Clouds swallowed up the bright stars. Animals sniffed the air in the Tumbling Wood, and Owly hooted ominously above the dark trees. Inside his burrow the Welsh Rabbit shivered and thought enviously of Mr Rab sleeping in Thomas's warm bed.

Tamworth awoke and went to look out of the window. Pigs always know when the wind is rising. Tamworth couldn't actually see the wind as some old country folk say that pigs can, but he felt strange and restless. At the farm, Mr Baggs muttered to himself in his sleep and somewhere a dog howled. At last Tamworth turned back to his own bed.

Melanie, too, was listening to the wind. Tamworth thought about the earth around him and all its problems but Melanie thought about her piglets, and most of all about Michael, the one she loved the best, and Ethel, because she was the one who got hurt. Albert will always be all right, she thought before she drifted off to sleep again. Albert will see that Albert is all right.

Mrs Twitchie lay awake for some time, and finally got up to make herself a pot of tea. She'd had a nasty nightmare about that Thomas child soon after she'd gone to bed and had been unable to go to sleep after it. She heard an owl hoot twice, so she took her tea back to bed and drank it there.

Lurcher Dench was playing football in his dreams, and was just about to shoot when he kicked his brother, Crasher, who slept with him. Crasher woke up and kicked him back and they had a fight before they went to sleep again.

The dream thoughts of Mrs Baggs were dark and formless and horrid. Tamworth wandered through them and so did Thomas, both of them laughing. She did not like that laughter. She felt angry, and snarled into Mr Baggs's ear. He moved over to the edge of the bed. Now hordes of laughing pigs were running everywhere, filling all the corners of Mrs Baggs's mind. She groaned in her sleep.

Blossom dreamt that she was in a wood, and there, hanging from the branches on coloured ribbons, were boxes of chocolates with her name on them. But suddenly she was surrounded by a crowd of thin hungry children, so she gave the boxes to them. The children went away, leaving her with just one box, and she was about to open it when she saw a waif-like little girl, crying pitifully, so she gave her the last box. Blossom whimpered in her sleep, for those boxes had been beautiful . . . but then she walked on in her dream, until she came to her world, the world she visited nearly every night, though she did not always remember it, the world that made her, or helped to make her, such a happy person in the daytime, and this world was full of music and trees and flowers and butterflies and strange, gentle creatures and changing colours. Blossom snuggled deeper into her pillow and smiled.

Outside the wind dropped a little, and from the dark sky, the snow began to drift down, small, round flakes at first, then larger and larger, flying and falling on to the frozen earth. Mr Rab shivered and snuggled nearer to Thomas. Hedgecock snorted loudly and settled deeper into his blanket of coloured squares.

And that snort woke up Thomas. The room was dark and he lay and thought about Christmas and what presents he was going to have—new football and kit and a box of chocolates, he hoped—and he remembered the funny present he'd bought for his sister, and grinned to himself in the dark and started to doze off, when he heard the church clock strike one . . . two. . . . And he was instantly wide awake and ravenously hungry. It was terrible. He tried to curl up in a ball round his stomach but it was no good. The pangs of hunger were dreadful. He must have something to eat or he would die there in bed. He could see the headlines in the paper—

TERRIBLE TRAGEDY
Boy found dead in bed just before Christmas

Parents heartbroken. Starvation suspected. Famous Pig to dress all in black for funeral.

Thomas, by now almost believing that he was really starving, pushed his feet out of the bed and felt for his slippers, his old ones, hoping as he did so that slippers wouldn't be one of his presents as that was the kind of present he hated and he'd already got that awful pullover from Aunt Cynthia. This reminded him that he must be careful not to wake her or anyone else. He opened the bedroom door, and tried his torch, but the battery had gone, so he crept down in the dark. It was warmer in the kitchen and he felt very happy as he began his grub search. It took him a while, but eventually he sat down with two cream crackers, three mincepies, a cold potato, a piece of cheese and a packet of peanuts. He found an old paperback, a collection of ghost stories, and was soon lost in adventure, munching away, showering bits on the floor. When he'd finished he rummaged in the pantry again, and came out with an orange, another piece of cheese and a glass of milk. Spilling half the milk and dropping the orange peel on the floor he settled down again for another story. It was an especially frightening one, and just as he finished it, a gust of wind blew suddenly with a strange howling noise. It startled Thomas and he jumped up, book falling to the floor with a bang. Thomas, afraid that he was about to be visited by ghosts at any minute, wanted the safety of bed and the comfort of Num, his blanket, very badly. He shot out of the kitchen and up the stairs, back to safety.

Unfortunately, such was his speed that he tripped on the top stair, lost his balance and fell, bump, bump, bump, hitting every stair with some bit of him.

"Ow! Ow! Oweerrrhhhh!" he yelled.

"Jeffrey!" shrieked a voice. "Wake up! Burglars!"

Lights went on and a low grumbling rumble showed that Uncle Jeff was waking to Aunt Cynthia's call. The landing light was switched on, and there stood Blossom, rubbing her eyes.

"Thomas has gone. He isn't in his bed," she said.

"Gone?" cried her mother, just appearing on the landing. "Where's he gone?"

"Burglars!" shrieked Aunt Cynthia in the doorway. "Don't panic. I've got a weapon!"

She was waving a large flower vase in the air. From

the direction of the hall a sad, moaning noise could be heard.

"Put that thing down," shouted Uncle Jeff, joining the gathering on the landing, and trying to get the vase away from Aunt Cynthia.

"What on earth is going on?" growled a voice that resembled an angry Polar bear woken from a deep sleep to an Arctic dawn. Dad had arrived.

"Burglars have kidnapped Thomas!" cried Aunt Cynthia.

By now, Blossom, realising where the wailing noise was coming from, had rushed downstairs, followed by her mother.

"Of course burglars haven't kidnapped Thomas," shouted his father furiously. "First of all, no burglar would ever want Thomas, and secondly, he's there, at the bottom of the stairs, making that awful racket."

"Oh poor Thomas," comforted Blossom.

"My poor lamb," cried his mother.

"Poor nothing," bellowed his father. "What I want to know is what he's doing out here in the first place?"

He ran down the stairs, where Thomas was investigating himself to discover how many bones he had broken. Then he looked into the kitchen.

"And what's all that mess in there?" he asked.

Thomas gave a groan of despair.

"I might just as well be dead or in a dungeon," he cried.

Chapter Nine

Thomas awoke, stretched out his legs in bed and wondered why he ached so much. Practically every bit of him seemed to be creaking and groaning. Then he remembered the night before and falling downstairs. No wonder he felt sore. The stairs had felt very hard indeed. He moved again cautiously this time. Why, he must be absolutely covered in bruises. He thought about this, lying still and looking up at the ceiling. And the ceiling looked somehow different. He didn't know why or how, but definitely different, somehow strange; in fact, there was a strange feeling about his room altogether, and that wasn't just because Blossom was in the camp bed in his room while Uncle Jeff and Aunt Cynthia were staying— no, he'd got used to that, even though he didn't like it. What was it? Something about the light and the way it came through the curtains. Stiffly, he got out of bed and limped towards the window, pulled aside the curtains and peered out—

"Yippee," he yelled at the very top of his voice, then, "Yippee," and "Yippee" again.

For his entire world lay blanketed in snow, and not just a little, thin, tiny layer of snow, but snow inches thick, deeper than Thomas had ever seen, covering up everything, the garden, the path, the plants, the hedge, roofs, roads, in the whitest of whites ever seen, pure white, untouched by foot or hand, by anything, in fact, except delicate bird tracks, just waiting for Thomas to get at it, hold it, throw it, roll in it, slide on it, make snowballs out of it, snowmen out of it.

He couldn't wait to get dressed. Grabbing clothes, he rushed round the room, bruises forgotten. He threw Hedgecock and Mr Rab out of bed, crying, "It's come, it's come." They immediately tried to get back in bed again.

By now, Blossom was stirring, and pushing her nose out of the warm covers like a sleepy mole.

"Wh-what did you say?" she asked, yawning.

Thomas took a running jump on to her bed.

"You beast, mind my tum," she shrieked.

"It's snowing. It's snowing and it's deep. Come on. Get up. Come and look."

"Snow! Let me see."

She ran to the window and gazed at the world she knew, changed out of all recognition overnight.

"It's so beautiful," she whispered.

By now Thomas was dressed in a scrambled sort of fashion and jumping downstairs two at a time.

"I don't want any breakfast," he said, in the doorway of the kitchen.

"Oh, yes, you do. This is just the time that you do want a good breakfast inside you. So, just get on with it."

Actually, Thomas found no difficulty at all in eating

his way through porridge, scrambled egg and fried potato, followed by strawberry jam on toast, and an orange. Once or twice Aunt Cynthia, nibbling a crispbread, shuddered slightly, especially when he popped a little jam on his egg just to see how the two went together. Armed for the day, he stood up to go. His father loomed in the doorway, wearing a duffel coat and wellingtons and carrying a spade.

"Dad, isn't it fantastic?"

"I fail to share your enthusiasm. I have been up for two hours endeavouring to clear the road so that I can get to work. It will be cold and uncomfortable. Old people will die of pneumonia and young children will catch cold. The life of the country will be disrupted. On the other hand," and he grinned widely, "hop out and enjoy yourself as much as you can while it lasts."

"Thanks, Dad."

He was out of the house and on his way to see Tamworth just as Blossom arrived for her breakfast. It was hard work walking along, Thomas found. The snow came nearly to the tops of his wellingtons. He picked some up and made a snowball. His fingers tingled—he hadn't wanted to wear gloves. He threw the snowball at a tree and watched it splat against the trunk. Then he trekked along the path, loving the feeling of being the first to tread there. He looked behind and there he could see his footsteps in the snow behind him, the ridges on his wellingtons showing up clearly. He felt like a path-finder, an explorer . . . He bent down and signed his name and looked at it with pride. Near Pig House, the snow was deeper, for it had drifted with last night's wind.

It came over his wellingtons and settled down squashily on to his socks. He didn't mind.

Tamworth was busy clearing the snow from the front of Pig House, glowing red-gold with exercise. Melanie was throwing some food for the birds.

"Poor things, they will be so hungry," she said.

"Come on, Thomas, somewhere at the back of the shed there's a toboggan. Let's have a look for it."

They searched among the old picture frames, pieces of hardboard, tin cans, bicycles, old television sets, and cardboard boxes and there it was, in good order except that one of the runners was a bit loose. But Thomas fixed it because Tamworth wasn't handy with his trotters, he said with a grin.

They decided to go to the Common, where there was a fairly steep slope, and the toboggan would go with a fair amount of speed. Melanie busily packed a bag with some grub and a first-aid kit, if needed. No, she didn't want to have a ride, but she would like to watch. Pulling the sledge, they set off.

"Wait for me," cried a voice, and Blossom, her face as scarlet as her woolly hat, ran after them. Thomas couldn't resist such a target. A well-aimed snowball knocked off the hat.

"Take that," she yelled, and threw one in return, which missed Thomas but flew straight into Tamworth's ear.

"Ouch," yelped Tamworth, his ear twitching wildly. He hurried back to the house, to return wearing a muffler wrapped round his ears and looking most peculiar.

At last, they reached the Common, where the Dench brothers were already speeding down the hill, on a contraption created from corrugated iron. They watched as Crasher and Lurcher sped stylishly with a splendid curve down to the bottom of the slope. Thomas watched a little enviously while Blossom was privately rather scared.

"I'll watch you, first," she said, sitting on a tree-trunk beside Melanie.

Tamworth placed his huge form carefully on the sledge, then Thomas got on behind, holding tight. Someone gave them a push and down the slope they went, the wind whistling past their ears and whipping their faces. Thomas felt that he was nearer to flying than he'd ever been before. In no time at all, they were near the bottom. Tamworth shouted something but Thomas couldn't hear. The sledge swerved, Tamworth sat tight, but Thomas shot off and rolled in the snow, roaring with laughter. They made their way back up to the top again,

just in time to see Blossom, a terrified look on her face, being whirled away by Lurcher, performing in top Dench style. He brought the sledge beautifully to a halt after a perfect curve. Blossom was beaming now, and ready for more turns.

Henry next appeared with his father, the Professor. They had brought along an almost antique model, very handsome indeed. Tamworth and Thomas went over to inspect this fine specimen.

"We found it in the loft," explained Henry. "There's lots of old junk up there."

That particular piece of old junk went splendidly, the Professor sitting bolt upright on it, long beard tucked in his jacket.

Tamworth and Thomas learned to manoeuvre quite well with some practice, then Tamworth announced that he must simply have some refreshment as he was losing vast amounts of weight through all this exercise. So Melanie brought apples and crisps and biscuits out of her bag and a cabbage for Tamworth. Then Mrs Dench turned up with a huge bag of sandwiches, and Mummy with hot drinks in three thermos flasks.

"What a jolly occasion this is," cried Tamworth, and everyone agreed.

Thomas, however, was watching Lurcher, who appeared to be showing off.

"I'm the best, the greatest," he was announcing to Blossom, who sat there with an admiring expression on her face. This was too much for Thomas, who crept up behind and stuffed snow down the back of his neck.

"Ouch!" yelled Lurcher, jumping up hurriedly, and

leaping round to see who had done it. Within seconds he and Thomas were rolling, scrapping, pushing snow into each other's faces, both of them full of fury and joy. They did enjoy fighting each other, for no one else could fight so well.

And somehow, without anyone knowing how or where or when, a colossal snowfight started, with snow-balls flying through the air, and everyone shrieking and hurling, "Take that, and that!" and people falling and laughing and getting up to throw another one, and every-one warm and covered in snow.

At last the fight stopped almost as suddenly as it had begun. It was time to go homewards. They trailed along together, dragging their sleds, singing "Jingle Bells" and vowing to return in the afternoon for more tobogganning.

After lunch, Thomas went off again, but Blossom stayed behind in the front garden to carry out an idea of her own. A quantity of unused snow lay there, and she first of all gathered together a great pile of the lovely white stuff. Then she firmed it into a column, taller than herself. The snow was just right for doing this, not too fine and powd-ery, and it stuck well. Then she methodically rolled a large snowball and placed it on top of the column for the head. All this was hard work on her own, and she was puffing and panting, but very happy. She wanted to surprise everyone with what she had made. She placed a large black hat of her father's, an old one, on the snow-man's head, and put in two stones for eyes. A carrot served as a nose. The mouth was more difficult. She put in a small piece of twig and an old clay pipe she'd had years ago for blowing bubbles. Two large sticks served as arms with two old gloves of Thomas's hanging on the ends. Finally she put a woolly scarf round the snowman's neck.

"That'll keep you warm," she said, patting him, and arranging a row of pebbles down his front for buttons. There, he was finished.

Then she called Mummy, Aunt Cynthia and Uncle Jeff.

"I want you to meet Mr Fred Snow," she said and bowed.

They all clapped, and Blossom jumped up and down, saying:

"He's a very nice person and he's going to stay with us a long time."

Funnily enough, when the snow melted Mr Fred Snow was the last heap to go. He stayed longer than any of the rest, together with some pebbles, some twigs and a hat.

"Come on, Blossom. Tamworth's on telly," called Thomas, grabbing Hedgecock and Mr Rab and throwing himself down before the fire.

"But he can't be," Blossom said, puzzled.

"Why not?"

"Because he's here. Or, I mean, he's been here all day, in the snow, so he wouldn't have time to get to the television studios, especially in this weather."

"It's pre-recorded, stupid. He did it last week. In fact, he's going to watch it himself at home."

"How peculiar," thought Blossom, but she didn't wish to be called stupid again, so she kept quiet.

Tamworth's face appeared on the screen, looking exceedingly golden and handsome on the new colour television set. He told a story about a miser pig, who learned to be generous at Christmas time, because he was frightened by a ghost pig.

"That story sounds like one I know," Daddy grinned.

"I liked that miser pig," Hedgecock said. "A very sensible animal, I thought he was. I don't see why he had to change his ways."

"Huh," sniffed Mr Rab moving away in disgust.

"Sh." Tamworth was looking straight at the viewers.

"Isn't it funny that he can't see us, when he appears to be here in this room, with us?"

"Shut up," growled Thomas.

Tamworth smiled his curly grin at the audience, then began to speak very seriously and gently.

"Christmas is a time for loving, a time for friendship and laughter. And many of us are lucky enough to share our Christmas Day with those we love. But there are those who are not happy at Christmas time; people and animals who are alone, poor, friendless, homeless. And to them, this season of Christmas is made even more wretched by seeing others enjoying themselves, so that they feel even more unwanted. To these lonely ones I stretch out my trotters in welcome. Come to me. Come to Pig House. Anyone at all, two-footed or four-footed, who feels lost and alone, will be made part of a family with me at Christmas, this year."

The huge grin widened and widened until it filled the whole television screen.

"Good night," he said, and his ears pricked up and then he was gone.

"That was wonderful," Blossom sighed.

"I'm not at all sure about that," muttered Hedgecock. "I wouldn't want all the lonely people and animals coming here. Where should we put 'em all? How should we feed 'em? No, I think Tamworth has bitten off more than he can chew, this time."

"I don't agree," cried Mr Rab and they went arguing up to bed.

Thomas, worn out with all the excitement of the day, fell asleep, snuggled into Num.

Chapter Ten

Christmas Eve had arrived, at last. Thomas and Blossom arose early and looked out of the window to see if the snow had disappeared overnight. It hadn't, so they privately examined the presents they'd bought for other people and hid them safely away again.

Mr Rab managed to sing "Jingle Bells" all the way through before Hedgecock woke up.

"Grrrh," he snarled, pulled the blanket of knitted squares over his head and went back to sleep again.

"I've made up a carol of my own," said Mr Rab, wistfully. "Do you think you'd like to listen to it, some time?"

"Of course we would," Blossom cried, picking up the small animal and hugging him. "When do you want to sing it to us?"

"Tonight. Last thing before we go to sleep, and then when we wake up we'll find it's Christmas Day."

"Tonight, then. We'll have a sing-song together."

"*He* won't like it." Mr Rab indicated Hedgecock, who made a snorting noise at that moment.

"*He* can lump it, then," said Blossom, sounding like her mother.

They went downstairs ready and eager to help with everything, even Thomas, for this was Christmas Eve, so jobs were special somehow, even something ordinary like fetching the loaves, because there'd be several days afterwards when you couldn't fetch them. Thomas actually carried Aunt Cynthia's bag for her and helped her across the street, which was full of dirty, sloshy, brown stuff that had once been snow. The roof-tops were still sparkling white, however, under the blue sky.

"I think you're growing to be a better boy," said his aunt to Thomas.

"You've just got to be joking," Blossom muttered, but Aunt Cynthia didn't hear, fortunately.

Next, they checked the Christmas tree, to see that the lights were working properly, and they added a few more chocolate decorations that they'd just bought. Then they blew up the balloons, which tend to go down if they're done too early, and Dad, who was at home, fixed them on the ceiling. They had a game with the last one, hitting it as hard as possible until it finally burst on a holly prickle. They hung the mistletoe in the hall, and Dad kissed Aunt Cynthia under it, which made her giggle. This greatly astonished Thomas.

"I didn't know that anyone could actually kiss her, you know," he remarked to Blossom. As he had thought so often before, grown-ups were really most peculiar. Still, as long as he wasn't expected to kiss anyone, they could do what they liked, he supposed.

"I shall kiss Lurcher," said Blossom, dreamily.

Thomas made his sick noise, which his mother, just coming in, heard in its full glory.

"Thank you for your help. You can go and play now, if you like."

If you like means that she wants you to, thought Thomas, but he got out his wellingtons readily and he and Blossom set off for Pig House through the snow.

Quite a crowd had gathered at the slope, making the most of the snow before it melted. Some people were getting really skilled in handling their sledges now, notably Crasher and Lurcher Dench.

"Lurcher's good enough for the Olympics," sighed Blossom, but Thomas didn't hear, which was just as well. He and Tamworth had had one or two good runs when he looked up to see Christopher Robin Baggs and Gwendolyn Twitchie approaching. She was wearing a fur-trimmed, embroidered red jacket and hood, with matching mittens, which was immediately the envy of every girl there. But what the boys looked at was Christopher Robin's brand new sledge with shining steel runners.

They both looked around them. A silence fell.

"I suppose it will have to do," Gwendolyn said, at last.

"Better than nothing," agreed Christopher Robin, shrugging his shoulders.

They took their turn to go down the slope. Thomas hoped they would crash in a heap but they didn't. They sailed down rather sedately, and made their way back up again as if they found it all rather boring.

And, somehow, much of the pleasure left the rest of them. The magic had gone. The slope wasn't very steep after all, and the sledges were a funny, shabby lot. Lurcher messed up a curving run and landed in a heap, but no one laughed. It was cold and the sky slowly turned from blue to grey and it began to snow again, little nasty flakes. Thomas shivered. He felt hungry too, and today there was no Melanie with a bag full of grub, nor Mummy with hot drinks nor Mrs Dench with food for all her sons and anybody else if they wanted it. It was, after all, Christmas Eve and they were very busy.

At last, Thomas had to do something, so he hurled a snowball at Christopher Robin Baggs. It missed and hit Gwendolyn instead. She shook off the snow and looked at Thomas with disdain.

"I might have known that you would do that," she said. "You always did spoil things. Come along, Chrissy. Let's go home."

And they turned to go, but Blossom shot forward, face as red as her woolly hat.

"It wasn't Thomas who spoiled it," she cried. "It was you, you stuck-up prig!"

Gwendolyn merely tossed her yellow curls and walked on, her spotty friend a few yards behind. It was clear that Blossom was near to tears and Tamworth went up to her and put a kindly trotter on her arm. He was just about to speak when everything erupted around them. Noise everywhere, squeals, shouts, laughter and—

"Dad! Dad! Thomas! Blossom! Everybody! Look! Look! Look! I've come. Albert's here. Albert's come. And the others. Can I have a go? Which is the best sledge? Thomas, give me a go. Dad! We've come. Merry Christmas, everybody!"

Blossom's tears vanished. "Merry Christmas," cried everyone. No one minded the cold. Nothing mattered except that Albert was back (and of course, his brothers and sisters, though that wasn't quite as important, not to Albert, anyway) and Christmas was coming. Up and down the slope they flew. Snowballs soared through the air. Piglets and children rolled and laughed and screamed.

"But you're so big, Albert," cried Blossom.

"Albert extremely large and handsome pig," he agreed.

"Ethel, you've grown, too."

"Ethel very pleased to see Albert," stated that pig.

Ethel wasn't so sure about this. She now had a comfortable home with a kind family but sometimes she had a nightmare where Albert was pulling her tail or sitting on her or performing some other kind, brotherly act. Yet Albert, grinning, was irresistible. So she smiled at him, and Blossom flung her arms round his neck, saying how wonderful it was to see him again.

"It's time to go back home," cried Tamworth, looking proudly at his large family gathered around him. They'd grown into fine pigs.

"We're off, now," they called to the others. "Cheerio," and accompanied by Thomas and Blossom they returned to Pig House.

By the time they were almost there, the snow was falling in earnest and it was difficult to see far ahead of them. It appeared to be growing dark extra early as well.

"What a perfect Christmas Eve," sighed Blossom.

"Yes, but it's very dangerous for those who have to travel far," replied Tamworth, a worried note in his voice.

"Yes, all our family aren't here yet. Only sixteen of us," replied Michael, the eldest son.

"I do hope that everyone reaches his destination safely tonight," Tamworth said, very seriously indeed.

As they approached Pig House, they could see that the snow had been trampled down all around, though the falling snow was rapidly covering the tracks. Dark shapes could be seen walking through the snow, and dark figures were standing in the porch.

"Whoever can they be?" asked Tamworth.

Blossom said nothing. She felt too cold. But she felt sure she knew who they were. And Melanie ran towards them, wrapped in a shawl, panting hurriedly.

"Tamworth, my dear, they keep coming and coming—dozens of them—coming and coming all afternoon—Mrs Baggs has already been to complain to me because they keep going across her land and calling at the farm and asking where Pig House is, and she's furious—and they're all so cold, poor dears—if only it would stop snowing..."

"And if only you would stop talking, my dear, and tell me what is happening," Tamworth interrupted.

"They keep coming and coming ..."

"Who keep coming and coming ...?"

"Homeless people and animals. Dozens of them. Saying you'd invited them."

And the full truth dawned upon Tamworth and he realized just what he'd done.

"Dear me," he said, in consternation. "Dear, dear me."

Chapter Eleven

It was the Vicar's wife who saved the day. She arrived post haste after Tamworth had despatched Thomas and Blossom to fetch her, and she took one look at the pathetic collection of bedraggled people and animals and promptly took charge.

"The Church Hall is the place. Room for dozens of people in there. Tamworth, you attend to the heating, and see how many men you can get to call in there. Blossom and Thomas, ask the ladies of the village, your mother, Mrs Postlewaithe, Mrs Dench, Mrs Twitchie..."

"I'm not asking her anything," said Thomas.

"Then I will, and Aunt Cynthia," promised Blossom.

"... and anyone else you can get to come. Ask them to go to the Church Hall, and to beg, borrow, or steal food, beds, sleeping bags, cups, saucers, plates, hay, buckets, first aid, anything. And now, all you piglets, oh, my, aren't you all grown up? I should never have known you. Well, you take all of them down to the Hall and look after them till we can all get there. Right?"

"Right," everyone agreed.

And so it was that, some hours later, despite the dark, the falling snow, and people having jobs to do in their own homes, the Church Hall was full of furniture, decorated with balloons and paper chains. A tree stood in the corner, with a present on it for everyone. Aunt Cynthia and Blossom had toiled non-stop wrapping all the gifts that people had given. Thomas and Henry took everyone's name and made a long list. A tea urn was set up in one corner, with a barrel of beer from the Duck and Drake and a barrel of cider from Farmer Baggs, who had also donated loads of animal fodder. This had made Mrs Baggs incredibly angry, as she hated giving anything away. Mummy and Mrs Postlewaithe made soup in a bath and great piles of sandwiches. The Dykes had given all the bread left over in the shop. Daddy fixed up a television set in another corner and a microphone for the evening's concert. For it had been decided that there was to be a concert, with Mrs Twitchie in charge. She was bustling about, full of bounce. Thomas kept out of her way. Mr Starling had put a splint on a badger with a broken leg, and combed a very old sheep dog that had undergone terrible treatment somewhere. It seemed that all the village had something to spare and was ready to give. Even Deadly Dench, who had recently formed his own group, volunteered his latest number, entitled, "My baby has the slouchin', grouchin' blues," for the concert. This remarkable offer was received with no enthusiasm at all by some people present, but both Tamworth and the Vicar's wife, being more generous-hearted, felt that all offers should be gratefully accepted.

But just as Tamworth and the Vicar's wife were taking a well-earned breather and a cup of tea, Mrs Baggs appeared in the doorway, eyes wild, hat askew, snowflakes melting all over her.

"Shameful, 'tis. Shocking. People knocking on my door all day long, ruining my garden, giving me no peace. Beggars and tramps and such-like, and disgusting animals, traipsing over the countryside, upsetting decent people, law-abiding folk. I don't know what the country is coming to. And that Farmer Baggs, that ought to know better, giving away stuff that we can ill afford, and without my say-so as well. It'll be your fault—" she turned on Tamworth—"I heard that fulish broadcast of yourn, if this village is ruined or burnt down in the night. And you—" she turned to the Vicar's wife—"you sinful woman . . ."

"Oh, do come in and have a cup of tea," said that sinful woman.

"Or a glass of port," suggested Tamworth. "But please close the door," for the snow was swirling in.

"Don't you try to tempt me. Or to get me away from what I want to say. Who are all these creatures, I want to know . . . ?"

"God's creatures," said the Vicar's wife, but Mrs Baggs wasn't listening.

". . . Spies, traitors, hijackers, terrorists, are they? Shall we all be blown up or murdered in our beds?"

"I don't think it likely with the poor things who've come here," Tamworth said, "though I could get P.C. Cubbins to check them all for weapons. He's busy with the crackers at the moment."

"The whole world's gone mad and it's all your fault, Tamworth Pig, cluttering up my dreams with your wickedness and laughter . . ."

"What?" cried Tamworth, genuinely astonished by now.
The Vicar's wife said firmly:

"Please come in and close the door, for it's cold and
you don't look at all well."

"And if I don't look at all well, whose fault is it?
First I have nightmares about Tamworth Pig, and then
he brings half the thieves, rogues and vagabonds in the
country here, to our village. I'll set the police on to you,
that I will."

"Well, you can't," said Tamworth, somewhat sharply,
"because they are already here, helping."

Mrs Baggs shook her fist at him and then at everyone
in the Hall and rushed forth into the night, into the snow
and cold. The Vicar's wife ran after her, putting a hand
on her arm to stop her, but Mrs Baggs shook her off,
shouting:

"Leave me alone."

Tamworth and the Vicar's wife looked at each other
with anxious eyes, then turned and went back into the
Hall.

The concert was a huge success. Nothing like it had happened before. Tired Mums laughed and sang and forgot
what they were supposed to do for a while; children
waiting for a Christmas morning that never, never seemed
to come, stopped counting the long hours. Dads enjoyed
the company and the refreshment. Deadly and his group
went down so well that they did another number,

"I'm a Market gardener looking for my carrot,"

which received riotous applause. Henry's father did

conjuring tricks and Mrs Dench danced a flamenco which nearly brought the stage down. Gwendolyn Twitchie recited a poem and Lurcher had to hold on to Thomas to stop him leaving. He also suffered when Uncle Jeff and Aunt Cynthia danced a tango. Uncle Jeff was one of the star turns of the evening, telling joke after joke, amid gales of laughter.

"I like this sort of thing," he said.

The piglets, now all safely arrived, sang:

"*Twenty fat piglets sitting on a wall,*"

and fell off the stage one by one. And Mrs Twitchie led the school orchestra in "The animals went in two by two." Very appropriate.

A reluctant Hedgecock had been taken along by Thomas, who carried him on to the stage, along with Lurcher and Henry.

"We've got Hedgecock's number trick for you," they announced. Everyone cheered.

"Think of a number, but don't say it out loud."

The audience thought of a number.

"Double it."

The audience did so, thinking hard.

"Add ten."

They added ten.

"Halve it."

They halved it. This took some people a bit longer.

"Now, take away the number that you first thought of and the answer is . . . Wait for it, everybody! The answer is . . . FIVE!"

"YES!" yelled the audience, who had all got the answer five.

"That's an old one," murmured Dad, grinning to himself.

"How did we all get five?" asked the Vicar's wife, puzzled. Thomas, Lurcher and Henry beamed with satisfaction.

"Aha," they said.

"I got three," whispered Mr Rab to Blossom.

"You did it wrong," she whispered back.

After a minute or two she went over to the Vicar's wife and consulted with her. The Vicar's wife nodded and went on to the stage, bearing a piece of paper.

"Here is a new carol, that I should like to sing specially for you," she smiled at the audience. And thus it was that

Mr Rab's carol was sung to a hall full of people after all. He hid his head against Blossom as the music started.

> *Softly, sing low,*
> *Low where a babe doth lie.*
> *Sweetly, sing sweet,*
> *Lest he should wake and cry.*
>
> *He comes to bring us light and joy.*
> *He is the one.*
> *He comes to bring us faith and love*
> *When hope has gone.*
>
> *Softly, sing low,*
> *Low where a babe doth lie.*
> *Sweetly, sing sweet,*
> *Lest he should wake and cry.*
>
> *He comes to ease a weary world,*
> *He is God's son,*
> *And Mary's boy will teach mankind,*
> *Just how God's will is done.*
>
> *Softly, sing low,*
> *Low where a babe has smiled;*
> *Sweetly, sing sweet,*
> *Sweet for a new-born child.*

When the Hall fell silent, Tamworth stepped forward.

"I want to thank everyone for helping, and everyone for coming. Merry Christmas!"

He bowed. The audience clapped.

"I'm dreaming of a White Christmas," sang the Vicar's wife.

"And you've got it, sister!" yelled Deadly, joining in with his group. "Everybody go! Go, cats, go!"

Going homeward at last, Blossom and Thomas were almost too tired to put one foot in front of another. But the snow had stopped and the stars were popping out one by one.

"What time is it?"

"Eleven o'clock. Only an hour to go."

"I can't wait," said Blossom.

"I can't wait," said Thomas.

But as soon as their heads touched their pillows, they fell fast asleep.

Chapter Twelve

Melanie and all the piglets were fast asleep, and Tamworth was just wondering whether he should lock the door of Pig House or leave it open for some late homeless arrival, when someone suddenly appeared.

"Who's that?" asked Tamworth.

" 'Tis I, Farmer Baggs. I want ee, Tamworth. I want ee to come with me. Nor do I want anybody to wake up."

They moved quietly away from Pig House and its sleepers. The stars were shining brightly now, and the snow crisping over.

"What's the matter? What are you doing out here?"

"Listen, Tamworth. Maud, Mrs Baggs that is, went out about nine o'clock and hasn't come back. And she's bin very funny lately, acting most peculiar-like. Bad dreams, she says, mind. And today, with all the a-coming and a-going, she said she was going right out of her head, like."

"I'm sorry," said Tamworth.

"Needn't be. She came back from the Church Hall, saw Christopher off to bed, she never neglects him whatever-come what may, and put his presents ready, then she turned on me, said everything was my fault, put on her hat and coat and went. And I thought she'd come back

87

when she got over it, but she didn't and she's out here still, in the cold. And I want ee to come and look for 'er wi' me, because I don't want anybody to know, specially at Christmas-time like. I don't mind ee knowing, Tamworth. Ee knows what's she's like, with her temper, but she'm me wife, for better or for worse and I've got to keep an eye to 'er."

"Wait a moment," Tamworth said. He went back to Pig House, and returned with a torch, his muffler, a bag with a small blanket in it and a bottle of brandy.

"I shall wear it under my chin, like a St Bernard dog," he thought.

Together they set out for the village, neither speaking, each lost in his own thoughts.

Tamworth felt tired, and his trotters were cold and aching. It had been a long day and all he wanted now was to sleep. The last thing he had any desire to do was to be out searching for Mrs Baggs. Memories of her flashed through his mind, and hardly any of them were pleasant. Her meanness with his food. Seizing Farmer Baggs's absence to try to get him slaughtered. Conspiring to get the motorway routed through Tumbling Wood. Little unkindnesses to the piglets as well as arranging their kidnapping. He really couldn't think why he was out and about on a cold and frosty night, looking for her, when he could be asleep in bed. And it was almost Christmas Day, and he wanted to enjoy Christmas Day, not search for a nasty woman who thought he was wicked. Then he looked at Farmer Baggs struggling along beside him, kind, reliable, and now looking tired and old,

and he knew that he could never refuse to help Farmer
Baggs.

There was no sign of her in the village, so on they went
to the Common. It was hard going in the snow and Tamworth felt that he would like just to lie down in it and go
to sleep. He sighed. Farmer Baggs sighed. The night was
quite light now, but it seemed completely empty of life.
Tamworth despaired of ever finding Mrs Baggs.

He turned to his companion.

"'This appears to be hopeless. There is no sign of her

anywhere, and it's like looking for a needle in a haystack. And for all we know she may be safely in someone's home."

"Please let's go on," said Farmer Baggs.

Tamworth's heart sank. Surely it would be better to tell the police? But he set out once more over the Common.

"Maud. Maud. Are you there?" called Farmer Baggs over the snow.

And at that moment the clock struck twelve and the church bells began to ring. It was Christmas Day.

And at that moment also, there came a great flurry and swirl of wings. Owly landed before them, blinking his round yellow stare.

"Follow me," he said.

On they stumbled after the owl, fluttering and swooping just ahead of them, right into Tumbling Wood, just as Tamworth somehow knew they would, to where the trees grew dark up to the dark sky.

Owly fluttered down.

"Indeed to goodness, it's a long time you've been a-coming," said the Welsh Rabbit. "Cold it is, hanging about here, and she too big to go into my burrow."

Mrs Baggs rested against a tree near to the elderberry bush. Seven or eight rabbits were by her side and on her lap.

"Keeping her warm, see," explained the Welsh Rabbit. "Not a very gracious lady, is she?" he whispered to Tamworth, who was busy getting the brandy and the blanket out of his bag.

The lady was speaking to Farmer Baggs.

"About time you got here," she shrilled at him.

"What have you bin up to, you fulish woman?"

"Twisted me ankle and can't walk. I was on me way to see me brother Bert. What 'ave you brought *him* for?" indicating Tamworth. "I'm having nothing to do with that pig . . ."

"Oh yes, you are." And picking her up, Farmer Baggs deposited her on Tamworth's back and wrapped the blanket around her.

"Madam, if you think this gives me any pleasure, you're very much mistaken," Tamworth muttered quietly under his breath.

"Take a swig of that," said Farmer Baggs, but she pushed the brandy away.

"I'll not 'ave that demon drink," she said.

"Yes, you will."

She took a look at his face and drank almost all the bottle. It made her gasp and then she remained quiet. The little rabbits still sat watching. Farmer Baggs picked up the Welsh Rabbit and stroked it.

"She would have died but for you and your friends. And though she is a fulish one, I thank you. I shall remember you. Goodbye."

The cold and the brandy combined to send Mrs Baggs fast asleep, and she snored as they went along. Farmer Baggs held her on.

And that was how Tamworth spent the early hours of Christmas Day. Walking in the snow with Mrs Baggs on his back.

And so came Christmas Day at last. People ate too much, drank too much, played games, watched television and snoozed. People received presents, some they wanted, some they didn't want. Dad had a pair of purple embroidered socks from Aunt Cynthia, that really surprised him; he only just managed not to shudder violently. Someone gave Tamworth a book on how to slim in a fortnight which he didn't care for at all. Thomas gave Blossom a Jack-in-the-Box which punched her when she opened it. She didn't find this particularly funny, but Thomas did. Mind you, he didn't think much of the Painting by Numbers she gave him, as he knew she really wanted to use it herself. But the best present of all went to Hedgecock, that meanest of animals, who didn't give anything to anyone. All his friends clubbed together to buy him an electric pocket calculator.

"That'll teach you to like Christmas," grinned Mr Rab, clutching his new book of poems to his narrow chest. And Hedgecock, rapturously working out the most incredibly difficult mathematical problems, didn't even bother to argue.

The visitors had a pleasant day, organized mainly by the Vicar's wife and Mrs Twitchie, who were busy sorting out both present and future problems. Mrs Baggs spent her Christmas in bed with a hangover. Tamworth, tired but content, was just about to fall asleep after the Queen's speech when he was struck by a sudden thought.

"Why, I meant to give up causes for Christmas. Instead I saved Mrs Baggs. Now that's a really splendid cause!"